The EAR BOOK

by Al Perkins

Illustrated by

WILLIAM O'BRIAN

A Bright & Early Book

DEFGHIJ   7890

Ears

Our ears

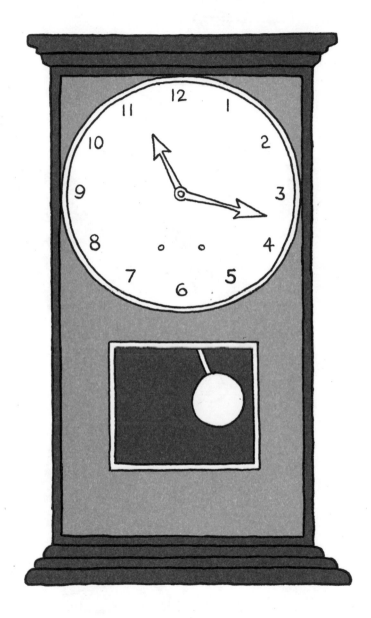

They hear a clock.

Our ears hear water.

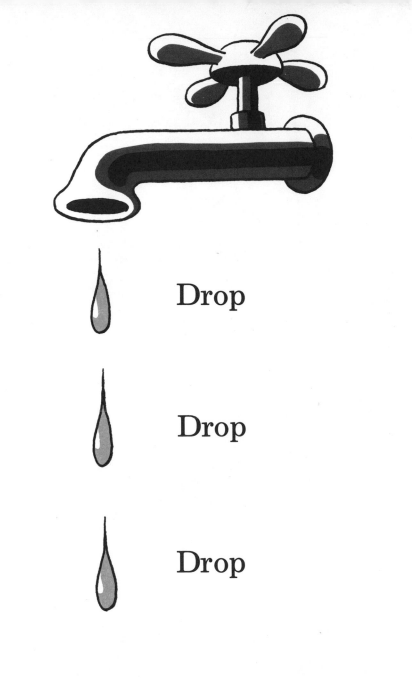

Drop

Drop

Drop

Our ears hear popcorn.

Ears Ears
Ears
Ears

It's good.
It's good
to hear with ears.

Toot
Toot
Toot

We hear a flute.

We hear a Ding.
We hear a Dong.

We hear a Ping.
We hear a Pong.

We hear my sister
sing a song.

We also hear
my father snore.

We hear my sister
slam the door.

Boom! Boom!
Boom! Boom!

Dum! Dum! Dum!

It's good
to hear
a drummer drum . . .

and sister blowing
bubble gum.

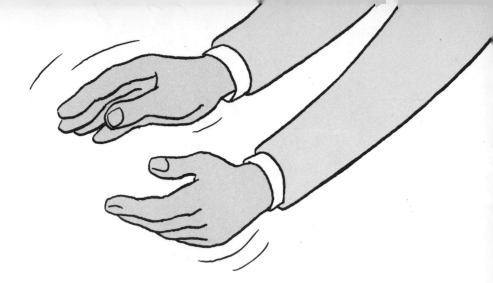

We hear hands clap

and fingers snap.

We hear feet
tap
tap tap
tap tap.

We hear a plane.

We hear a train.

It's good.
It's good
to hear the rain.

Ears. Ears. Ears!
We like our ears.
It's very good
to hear
with ears.